Falling
FOR THE FORBIDDEN
EX SEAL

Copyright © 2024 by Connie Blake

All rights reserved.

No portion of this book may be reproduced in any form without written permission from the publisher or author, except as permitted by U.S. copyright law.

CONTENTS

Introduction	V
1. Sarah	1
2. Ethan	6
3. Sarah	11
4. Ethan	19
5. Sarah	25
6. Ethan	30
Epilogue	34
7. Sneak Peak	38

INTRODUCTION

He's the one man I can't have. But the only one I want.

One reckless night with Ethan, my brother's best friend and ex-SEAL, changed everything.

He's all bad boy danger, dark smiles, with a body that should be illegal.

Walking away was supposed to be easy, but I can still feel his touch like fire on my skin.

Now I'm back. Running from a stalker ex and Ethan's the only one who can keep me safe.

Living under his roof, the heat between us is too much.

Every look, every accidental touch makes me want him more.

He says he'll protect me. But the way his eyes devour me,

the way his body brushes against mine, I wonder who's protecting who.

The need between us is electric and unstoppable.

One kiss, and I'm his.

If my brother ever found out how his friend handles my body, he would kill him!

It may be wrong, so why does his touch feel so right?

1

SARAH

The text came through just as I passed the 'Welcome to Fairhope' sign: *"You can't run forever."*

My heart clenched. My grip tightened on the steering wheel. Stewart wasn't done with me—not even close. After twelve hours on the road, I had hoped the distance would clear my head and keep me safe. I was wrong.

No matter how far I drove, he was always there. Lurking. Waiting. I thought Fairhope might be different. But as the pastel-colored buildings and oak-lined streets came into view, that same gnawing anxiety clung to me.

Stay calm, Sarah. Just breathe.

I pulled into the parking lot of the family bar, spotting Mark's truck—and next to it, a motorcycle. My stomach flipped. Ethan.

I hadn't expected to see him so soon. Or at all. Ethan, my brother's best friend, the guy I'd crushed on all through high school, even when Mark warned me to stay away. The same guy who'd been known around town for his wild streak—ditching curfews, racing his motorcycle through back roads, and leaving a trail of broken hearts. A bad boy with a grin that made girls swoon and guys jealous.

Mark had always made it clear: "Sarah, he's trouble. Don't even think about it." But one night, I didn't listen. One reckless night before we both left town—me for the city, and Ethan back to the Navy SEALs.

The SEALs had straightened him out, honed that raw energy into something focused, dangerous in a different way. But I knew Ethan still had that fire in him. It made him who he was, and back then, I'd been drawn to it like a moth to a flame.

I shook off the thought. Seeing him didn't matter. Not when Stewart was the real problem. My wrist still ached from where he'd grabbed me, his threats ringing in my ears.

Stewart had been so charming at first. Too charming. He knew exactly how to play the good guy—the cop everyone trusted. But behind the badge, he was something else. Dirty. Dangerous.

And now he was following me.

I parked, killed the engine, and took a deep breath. The bar looked the same, like a time capsule from my childhood. Mark was inside, and that should have comforted me.

But it didn't.

Because Ethan was inside too. And now, he was out of the military.

I stepped out of the car and adjusted the strap of my purse. The familiar scent of grilled food and old wood hit me as soon as I opened the door. Comforting. But it didn't loosen the knot in my chest.

I scanned the room. Mark was behind the bar, busy with a couple of regulars. He hadn't seen me yet. But then I spotted Ethan. He was leaning against the counter, broad shoulders relaxed, a beer in front of him. He looked the same as the day I left—strong, calm, the kind of guy who didn't have to say much to command attention.

My pulse quickened. I should have kept walking, made my way to Mark without being noticed. But my body had other ideas. I stood there, staring.

Then Ethan looked up.

Our eyes met, and for a second, the room seemed to fall away. All the memories of that night came rushing back. His hands on me, his mouth, the way he made me feel like I was the only woman in the world.

I swallowed hard, trying to regain control. I couldn't think about that now. Not with Stewart still out there.

Ethan raised an eyebrow, his gaze flicking from my face to the door, as if he already knew what I was thinking. Before I could move, he stood and started walking toward me.

"Sarah," he said, his voice low and calm, like nothing had changed between us.

But everything had changed. And I wasn't ready to face it.

"Ethan," I replied, forcing a smile that didn't reach my eyes.

He stopped in front of me, close enough that I could feel the heat radiating from his body. Too close. I fought the urge to step back.

"How long are you back for?" he asked, his eyes searching mine.

I opened my mouth to answer, but the words caught in my throat. How could I tell him the truth? That I was here to hide. That I had no idea how long I could stay, or if Fairhope would even be safe for me anymore?

"Just... for a while," I managed to say, my voice strained.

He didn't press, but his gaze lingered, like he could see straight through me. Like he could tell I was lying.

"You okay?" he asked, his voice softening. His concern felt too intimate, too familiar.

I nodded quickly, but my throat was tight. "Yeah, just tired. It's been a long drive."

Ethan glanced down at my wrist. The bruise was still faint but noticeable, and his eyes darkened.

"Sarah," he said, his voice dropping to a whisper. "What's going on?"

I pulled my hand back, hiding the bruise under my sleeve. "It's nothing. I'm fine."

But Ethan wasn't buying it. I could see the suspicion in his eyes. He took a step closer, lowering his voice even more. "Does Mark know?"

"No," I said quickly, shaking my head. "And he doesn't need to."

He stared at me for a long moment, his jaw tight. "Are you sure everything's okay? You don't seem like yourself."

The concern in his voice was almost enough to break me, but I couldn't let him in. Not yet. Not when everything was still too raw, too dangerous.

"I'm fine," I lied, forcing a smile.

The flicker of something unreadable crossed his face, but before he could respond, Mark's voice boomed from behind the bar.

"Sarah! You're back!"

I jumped, turning toward my brother. Relief washed over me like a wave. I needed the interruption.

Mark grinned, wiping his hands on a towel as he made his way over. He wrapped me in a bear hug, lifting me off the ground like he always did.

"Hey, big brother," I said, forcing a laugh as I pulled back.

"You didn't tell me you were coming," he said, his eyes flicking to Ethan, then back to me. "Everything okay?"

"Yeah, just decided to head back for a bit. Needed a break from the city."

"Well, it's good to see you," Mark said, his grin fading slightly as he studied my face. "You look... tired."

"I'm fine," I said quickly, glancing at Ethan, who was watching the whole exchange with a look I couldn't read.

Mark nodded, but I could tell he wasn't convinced. "Well, you know where to find me if you need anything. I'm here late tonight, but we'll catch up tomorrow."

I nodded, relief flooding through me. "Thanks, Mark."

I needed to get out of here. The tension was too thick, the weight of Ethan's gaze too heavy. But as I turned to leave, my phone buzzed again. My heart sank.

Another message.

You really think you can hide from me?

2

ETHAN

Fairhope was always quiet this time of night, a sleepy town where trouble rarely showed its face. That's what I loved about it. It was a far cry from the chaos I'd known in the Navy. No sandstorms, no gunfire, just the sound of crickets and the occasional bark of a dog in the distance.

But tonight, there was tension in the air. The kind of tension I couldn't shake. And it wasn't just the quiet or the small-town familiarity.

It was Sarah.

She'd walked into the bar earlier, looking like she hadn't slept in days. The bruise on her wrist—she tried to hide it, but I saw it. And something about the way she carried herself screamed danger.

I stepped out of the bar just in time to see Sarah heading toward her car, her head down, shoulders hunched like she was trying to make herself invisible. Mark was busy inside, but I couldn't ignore the tension rolling off her in waves. Something was wrong.

Seeing her like this stirred something in me, something I thought I'd locked away years ago.

I hadn't seen Sarah since that night. That one, unforgettable night years ago before she left Fairhope, when she was supposed to just be my best friend's little sister. It had been reckless, sure, but I couldn't stop myself back then. She had always been off-limits, someone I knew I shouldn't touch, but the attraction between us had been undeniable.

The night we spent together—it wasn't just physical. It felt like more, like something was beginning. But then she left. No warning, no explanation. I told myself I was fine with it. That I could move on, no harm done.

But seeing her here, in Fairhope again, after all these years? It brought all those feelings rushing back. The way she looked at me that night, the way we fit together so perfectly... I'd never been able to forget her.

And now, seeing her like this—scared, vulnerable—I couldn't just walk away.

I followed her out. Something was off.

"Sarah," I called after her, my voice calm but firm.

She flinched at the sound of my voice but didn't stop. I quickened my pace until I was next to her.

She glanced up, startled, her wide eyes betraying her nerves. "Ethan," she breathed. "What...what are you doing out here?"

"I could ask you the same thing," I said, crossing my arms. "You looked like you were in a hurry."

She shifted her weight from one foot to the other, avoiding my gaze. "Just tired. Long day."

I wasn't buying it. I saw the way her hands shook as she tried to fish her keys out of her purse.

When we reached her car, I froze. Her driver's side window was shattered, shards of glass scattered on the ground. And etched into the door in large, jagged letters was a word that made my blood run cold.

Mine.

My gut clenched. This wasn't random. Someone was sending a message.

Sarah stood frozen by her car, her eyes fixed on the vandalism like she couldn't believe what she was seeing.

"Sarah," I called, stepping forward. "What the hell happened here?"

Sarah's face paled, and she hugged her arms around herself. "I...I don't know. It was like this when I came out earlier."

I wasn't sure what infuriated me more—the thought of someone doing this or the fact that she hadn't told anyone. "And you didn't think to mention this to Mark? To me?"

Her lips trembled. "It's nothing. I'll take care of it."

"It's not nothing, Sarah." I turned to face her, my voice hardening. "Who did this?"

For a moment, she didn't answer. Her eyes darted away, her breath quickening. But then she exhaled, shoulders slumping. "It's Stewart."

The name hit me like a punch to the gut. Stewart. I'd never met the guy, but from what Mark had told me, Stewart was trouble—possessive, controlling. The kind of guy who didn't take breakups well.

"What's he doing here?" I asked, keeping my voice low.

She shook her head, her breath shaky. "We broke up a month ago. I thought he'd leave me alone, but he... he hasn't. He keeps showing up, sending messages, and now this."

A wave of anger surged through me. I'd seen this kind of thing before—guys who couldn't handle rejection, guys who thought they owned the women in their lives. It made my skin crawl. And now Sarah was caught in the middle of it.

I clenched my jaw, the protective instincts I'd honed over years in the SEALs kicking into overdrive. "And he's the reason you came back to Fairhope?"

She nodded, tears welling in her eyes. "I thought I could get away from him, but he's...he's always there. Watching. Waiting."

I couldn't believe this. She'd been dealing with this psycho for how long? And I hadn't known. "Why didn't you tell me sooner?"

"Because I thought I could handle it," she whispered, her eyes glistening with unshed tears. "I thought if I laid low, kept my distance, he'd move on."

I shook my head, stepping closer until I was standing right in front of her. "Well, that's clearly not working. You're not dealing with this alone, Sarah. You're staying with me tonight."

Her eyes widened. "Ethan, I—"

"No arguments," I said, my voice firm but gentle. "Mark's working late, and I'm not leaving you out here to deal with this by yourself. You'll stay at my place, and we'll figure this out in the morning."

The tension between us was thick, her hesitation palpable. But I wasn't giving her an out. She needed protection, and I wasn't about to let her push me away when she was in danger.

Her gaze flicked to my mouth, and before I could react, her lips were on mine.

The kiss wasn't gentle—it was fierce, desperate, a release of all the emotions we'd both been holding back. My hands found her waist, pulling her closer, deepening the kiss. Her hands gripped the front of my shirt, and for a moment, nothing else mattered. Not Stewart. Not the danger. Just her.

But then, just as suddenly, she pulled away, her breath coming in short, ragged gasps.

"We can't," she whispered, shaking her head. "I don't know what I'm doing."

"We'll figure it out later," I said softly, brushing a strand of hair behind her ear. "Right now, the only thing that matters is keeping you safe."

She nodded, biting her lip. "Okay. I'll stay."

I exhaled in relief, glancing back at her car. "I'll take care of this. But you can't be alone right now, understand?"

She nodded again, still looking dazed. I couldn't blame her. Her whole life had been flipped upside down, and now I was dragging her into mine.

But she wasn't alone anymore. Not while I was around.

As we made our way back to the bar to grab her things, I couldn't shake the feeling that this was far from over.

Stewart wasn't just some run-of-the-mill scumbag. He was a cop, and he knew how to stay out of sight.

But I'd been trained to track people like him. To find them. And if he was going to keep coming for Sarah, I'd be ready.

3

SARAH

Staying with Ethan felt both safe and dangerous. Safe because I knew he wouldn't let anything happen to me. Dangerous because every moment I was near him, I couldn't help but feel the pull—the connection that had been there since our one night together years ago.

I hadn't forgotten that night, no matter how hard I'd tried. The memory of Ethan—his hands on me, the way he kissed me like I was the only woman he'd ever wanted—had haunted me long after I left Fairhope.

That night had been a mistake, or at least that's what I told myself. I'd just wanted one night of passion before I left town to start a new life in the city. It wasn't supposed to mean anything. But it did.

When I met Stewart, I thought I was moving on, that I could forget Ethan. But Stewart wasn't Ethan. He was never Ethan. And now, being back here, under the same roof with Ethan again, I couldn't deny the pull between us.

Maybe I should be stronger. Maybe I shouldn't be doing this. I'd just gotten out of a toxic relationship. But Ethan wasn't like Stewart. He was the opposite—steady, calm, and dangerous in a way that made my heart race.

And maybe that's what I needed right now. To feel safe. To feel something real.

His short-term rental was small but cozy, tucked away on the outskirts of Fairhope. It was the perfect place to lay low while he figured out his next move, now that his time in the Navy SEALs was over and with no family left to return to. His parents had passed years ago, and with his only sibling moving across the country, Fairhope was the closest thing he had to home. After everything that happened, I needed to stay hidden, especially with Stewart getting closer. But being alone with Ethan brought up a whole new set of complications.

Ethan always had that edge—troublemaker in his youth, but the kind of guy who would give you the shirt off his back. He'd been reckless once, a bad boy who lived for speed, danger, and the thrill of the chase. Racing through town on his motorcycle, charming every girl, including me. But the Navy SEALs had changed him. Sharpened him. He came back with a new purpose, more discipline, but there was still that fire in his eyes. The one that had always drawn me to him, and now it burned hotter than ever.

"Make yourself at home," he said, tossing his keys on the kitchen counter. "I'm gonna lock up and change."

I nodded, wandering through the living room. The place was simple, yet warm, with soft lighting and a view of the woods from the back windows. The kind of place I could see myself writing. If only I wasn't trying to escape the mess my life had become.

I sank onto the couch, pulling my knees up to my chest. My mind raced, flipping between the last message I'd received from Stewart and the memory of Ethan's lips on mine in the parking lot. The kiss had been a mistake. I shouldn't have let it happen, but damn, it felt good.

The door clicked shut as Ethan came back inside, his presence filling the room.

"All secure," he said, his gaze settling on me. "You'll be safe here."

I forced a smile, but the weight of the situation pressed down on me. "Thanks, Ethan. For all of this."

He nodded, sitting down across from me. "You don't have to thank me. I told you, I'm not letting you deal with this alone."

His voice was steady, reassuring, but I couldn't shake the feeling that being here with him was more dangerous than facing Stewart. Not because I didn't trust Ethan—he was the one person I did trust—but because being close to him reminded me of how much I'd missed him. How much I'd never stopped wanting him.

"So," Ethan said, leaning forward slightly, "are you going to tell me the rest?"

I tensed, hugging my knees tighter. "The rest?"

"You mentioned you broke up. You didn't mention how bad it's gotten."

I hesitated. It was one thing to tell Ethan that Stewart was dangerous, but it was another to admit how deeply I'd let him into my life. How long I'd ignored the warning signs because I thought I could handle him. But I couldn't keep hiding the truth—not with Ethan involved now.

"He's a cop," I said, my voice barely above a whisper. "He's dirty. He's been dealing with criminals, making deals behind the scenes. I found out, and when I tried to leave, that's when he started coming after me."

Ethan's jaw tightened, his hands balling into fists. "And he's been following you ever since?"

I nodded. "At first, it was just messages, but then... the vandalism, the threats. He's trying to scare me."

"Sarah," Ethan said, his voice low and controlled, "he's not just trying to scare you. He's escalating. We need to stop this before it gets worse."

"I know," I whispered, my throat tight. "But I don't know what to do."

"You're doing the right thing by staying here," he said, moving to sit beside me on the couch. His closeness sent a shiver down my spine, and I had to remind myself to breathe. "We'll figure out the rest tomorrow. For now, you just need to rest."

"Can I take a shower?" I asked, standing abruptly. "I just...need to clear my head."

"Yeah, it's just through there," he said, pointing down the hall.

Ethan's gaze never left me as I moved toward the bathroom. "Take your time," he murmured, his voice low and rough, like gravel. There was a hunger in his tone, and I knew he was just as affected by our closeness as I was.

I closed the bathroom door behind me and leaned against it, my heart racing. What was I doing? Being here, with Ethan, after everything that had happened...it was dangerous. But the way my body reacted to him, the way my pulse quickened at his touch—it was undeniable. Irresistible.

I stripped off my clothes and stepped into the shower, letting the hot water cascade over me. But it wasn't enough to wash away the heat that had been building inside me since the moment I saw him again. Memories of our one night together flooded my mind—his hands on my body, his mouth on my skin. The way he had made me feel like the only woman in the world.

I shouldn't want him. Not now. Not after everything with Stewart. But my body didn't care about logic. It only cared about the way Ethan had once made me feel.

I turned off the water and wrapped myself in a towel, trying to regain control. But as I stepped out of the bathroom, I found Ethan standing by the window in the hall, his broad shoulders tense, his gaze focused on something outside.

"What is it?" I asked, my voice barely above a whisper.

He didn't turn around. "Just keeping an eye out. I don't trust Stewart. Not for a second."

I swallowed hard, stepping closer to him. "Ethan, you don't have to do this. I don't want you to get involved."

He finally turned to face me, his gray eyes burning with intensity. "I'm already involved, Sarah. I'm not going to let him hurt you."

His words hit me like a physical blow, knocking the air from my lungs. And before I could stop myself, I stepped closer, closing the distance between us. My towel slipped slightly, exposing the top of my breast, but I didn't care. All I cared about was the heat in Ethan's eyes, the way his body seemed to call to mine like a magnet.

"Sarah," he whispered, his voice rough with need, his gaze locked on mine.

I didn't give him a chance to say more. I pressed my lips to his, and the world around us disappeared. The kiss was fierce, hungry, a collision of all the emotions we had been holding back for so long. His arms wrapped around me, pulling me against him, and I felt the hard lines of his body through the thin fabric of his shirt.

The towel slipped away, leaving me bare against him, and Ethan's hands were everywhere—hot, urgent, exploring every inch of my skin. His mouth followed, kissing a path down my neck, my collarbone, lower... His teeth grazed the sensitive skin just above my breast, and I arched into him, a moan slipping from my lips.

"God, Sarah," he breathed, his voice thick with desire. "You're so beautiful."

I tugged at his shirt, desperate to feel his skin against mine. He pulled it over his head in one smooth motion, revealing the hard, chiseled muscles I remembered so well. My hands roamed over his chest, his abs, savoring the feel of him beneath my fingertips.

Ethan's mouth claimed mine again, more demanding this time. His hands slid lower, gripping my hips, and I could feel his arousal pressing against me through his jeans.

"I've wanted this for so long," he whispered, his lips brushing against my ear. "I've never stopped wanting you."

The words sent a thrill through me, igniting a fire that burned hotter than ever. I reached between us, unbuttoning his jeans, and Ethan groaned as I slid my hand lower, cupping him through the fabric.

"Sarah," he growled, his voice a low rumble in his chest. "I need you. Now."

With a swift motion, Ethan lifted me, my legs instinctively wrapping around his waist. He carried me to the bedroom, kicking the door open with his foot before laying me down on the bed. His eyes were dark, hooded with desire as he looked down at me, the tension between us crackling like fire.

I shivered at the feel of his hands on my skin, my body arching into his touch as he leaned down, his mouth trailing hot, open-mouthed kisses down my neck. His hands slid down my sides, gripping my hips, his fingers dipping under the waistband of his jeans as he quickly discarded them.

Then he was on me again, his skin against mine, his hands everywhere, leaving a trail of fire in their wake. I moaned, my body trembling with need as he kissed his way down my stomach, his breath hot against my skin.

"Ethan, please," I begged, my fingers tangling in his hair as his mouth hovered over my most sensitive spot, his tongue tracing a slow, teasing path.

He groaned against me, his hands gripping my thighs as he spread them wider, his mouth closing over me. I cried out, my back arching off the bed as he worked me with his mouth, his tongue swirling and teasing until I was on the edge of oblivion.

"Sarah," he rasped, his voice thick with desire as he slid up my body, positioning himself between my legs. "Tell me you want this."

"I want this," I gasped, my nails digging into his back as I wrapped my legs around his waist, pulling him closer. "I need you."

With one thrust, he was inside me, filling me completely. We both groaned at the sensation, the heat between us building until it was almost unbearable. He moved slowly at first, his hips rolling into mine in a rhythm that had me gasping for breath.

"Ethan," I moaned, my hands clutching his shoulders as he picked up the pace, driving into me harder, deeper, until I was trembling beneath him.

He leaned down, capturing my mouth in a searing kiss as his thrusts became more frantic, the tension between us building until it snapped. I cried out his name, my body shuddering as the waves of pleasure washed over me, taking me under.

Ethan followed soon after, his body tensing above mine before he collapsed, his breath coming in ragged gasps as he buried his face in my neck.

We lay there for a moment, our bodies tangled together, the heat between us still simmering.

"You okay?" he murmured, his voice soft, his fingers trailing lazily through my hair.

I nodded, unable to find the words. I wasn't just okay—I was more than that. For the first time in weeks, I felt...whole. Safe. And for now, that was enough.

"Sarah," he murmured, his lips brushing against my ear. "I'm not letting you go this time."

I smiled, my heart still racing as I wrapped my arms around him, pulling him closer. "I don't want you to."

4

ETHAN

It had been a few days since Sarah had moved in with me, and although I told myself it was for her safety, I couldn't ignore how right it felt to have her here. Every morning, I'd wake up to the scent of her lingering in the air, the warmth of her presence filling the house. But the more time we spent together, the harder it became to fight the desire that was constantly simmering between us.

That tension had only gotten worse since that night. Since we crossed the line that neither of us could ignore anymore. Now, it was like every touch, every glance, every accidental brush of our hands set a fire between us that was impossible to put out.

I couldn't stop thinking about her—how she looked in my bed, how she felt against me. But as much as I wanted to let that consume me, I couldn't forget the reason she was here. Stewart was still out there, and the threat he posed was too real, too close. I couldn't let my guard down. Not yet.

Mark hadn't said much, but I knew he was starting to suspect something was going on between us. The way he looked at Sarah whenever I was around... he wasn't stupid.

But I didn't have time to worry about that. Not when Stewart's threats were escalating.

I knew Sarah had a few hours alone to herself to work on her novel. But as I sat on the couch, trying to focus on the news, I couldn't help but notice the way her brow furrowed in concentration as she stared at her laptop. The way her fingers danced over the keyboard, her eyes bright with excitement one moment, then clouded with frustration the next.

I'd never seen her like this—so absorbed, so focused. It was clear she had poured her heart and soul into this story, and watching her work was mesmerizing.

"Everything okay?" I asked, trying to keep my voice casual as I leaned back on the couch.

Sarah looked up from her screen, her lips curving into a small smile. "Just trying to figure out where my characters are headed. It's a bit of a mess right now."

I chuckled, shifting slightly to get a better look at her. "Well, if they're anything like us, they're probably running around in circles."

She laughed softly, shaking her head. "Yeah, sounds about right."

There was a moment of silence as she glanced back at her laptop, then back at me, her eyes softening. "Ethan, I just... I want to thank you for everything. For letting me stay here. For... everything you've done."

I shook my head, dismissing the gratitude. "You don't have to thank me, Sarah. I told you I'd protect you, and I meant it."

She held my gaze for a moment, and something passed between us—an understanding, a connection that went deeper than just what we had physically shared. But before either of us could say anything, her phone buzzed on the table, and the tension in the room shifted immediately.

Sarah grabbed the phone, her face paling as she read the message.

"What is it?" I asked, my body already tensing.

She swallowed hard, holding out the phone to me. "It's from Stewart."

I took the phone from her, my jaw clenching as I read the text: *You think you're safe, Sarah? You're not. I'll always find you.*

My blood boiled. I wanted to find that bastard and put an end to this once and for all. But I knew we had to be smart about this. I couldn't let my emotions get the better of me. Not when Sarah's life was at stake.

"We need to report this to the police," I said, handing the phone back to her.

Sarah shook her head, her voice trembling. "He is the police. They won't do anything."

The frustration was building inside me, but I kept my voice steady. "We'll handle this, okay? I'll make sure you're safe."

She nodded, her eyes glistening with unshed tears. "I'm scared, Ethan."

I moved toward her, pulling her into my arms. She buried her face in my chest, her body trembling against mine. "I won't let anything happen to you," I whispered, kissing the top of her head. "Not while I'm here."

We stayed like that for a few moments, the weight of everything pressing down on us. I could feel Sarah's heartbeat racing against my chest, matching the storm of anger brewing inside me. But I knew we couldn't stay like this forever. Stewart was out there, and he wasn't going to stop until he got what he wanted.

As I pulled back slightly, something caught my eye through the window—a shadow, barely visible in the fading light. My entire body went still, instincts kicking in. Then I saw him. Stewart. Lurking at the edge of the woods like the coward he was. His eyes locked onto Sarah, a smirk playing on his lips.

Before I knew what I was doing, I was moving—putting myself between them, my body rigid with purpose.

"Sarah, stay inside," I said, my voice low and firm, the tone leaving no room for argument. "Lock the doors."

She stiffened beside me, her breath catching. "Ethan, what—?"

But I was already walking out the door towards Stewart. I could see the satisfaction in his eyes, the way he wanted to provoke me. To get a rise out of me.

"Nice place you've got here," Stewart called out, his voice dripping with mockery. "Didn't realize the great Ethan was playing house now."

I clenched my fists, resisting the urge to knock the smug grin off his face. "What the hell do you want, Stewart?"

He shrugged, taking a step closer. "Just checking in. Making sure Sarah's doing alright. I mean, she was mine not too long ago, wasn't she?"

That did it. Before I could stop myself, I lunged. I grabbed Stewart by the collar and slammed him against the nearest tree, my face inches from his.

"You don't get to talk about her like that," I growled. "And you sure as hell don't get to come near her."

Stewart just chuckled, his breath hot against my skin. "Oh, I'm shaking, Ethan. Really. But you and I both know this isn't over. She's not done with me yet."

I shoved him harder against the tree, but he didn't flinch. He just smirked, his gaze sliding past me to Sarah, who stood frozen a few feet away.

"You think you can protect her?" Stewart said, his voice low, almost amused. "You have no idea what's coming."

I forced myself to let go, stepping back as Stewart adjusted his collar, his smirk still in place. He looked at Sarah one last time before turning on his heel and disappearing into the woods.

I stood there for a moment, my fists still clenched, my heart pounding in my chest. The only sound was Sarah's ragged breathing behind me. Slowly, I turned around.

"Ethan," she whispered, her voice shaky. "He's not going to stop, is he?"

I took a deep breath, trying to steady myself. "No, he's not."

I closed the distance between us in two quick steps, wrapping my arms around her, holding her tight. She trembled against me, her fear so palpable I could feel it in my own bones.

"We'll figure this out," I murmured into her hair. "I promise. I'm not going to let him hurt you."

Sarah nodded against my chest, but I could tell she was still scared. And so was I. Stewart was playing a game, and I wasn't sure we were ready for his next move.

That night, I couldn't sleep. Sarah was lying next to me, her breathing soft and steady, but my mind was racing. I couldn't shake the image of Stewart's smirk, the way he'd looked at Sarah like he still owned her. Like he thought he could walk back into her life whenever he wanted.

I needed to stop him. But more than that—I needed Sarah to trust me. Fully.

As if sensing my thoughts, Sarah stirred beside me, her eyes fluttering open. She turned to face me, her gaze soft in the dim light.

"Can't sleep?" she whispered.

I shook my head. "Just thinking."

She reached out, her hand brushing against my arm. "About Stewart?"

"About you," I admitted. "About how scared I am that he's going to hurt you. And I don't know if I can protect you from him."

Her brow furrowed, and she shifted closer, her warmth seeping into me. "You've already done more for me than I ever expected, Ethan. You're the only one I trust right now."

I swallowed hard, the weight of her words settling over me. "Then let me protect you fully, Sarah. No more holding back. No more pretending you don't need help."

For a long moment, she was silent, her gaze locked on mine. Then, finally, she nodded, her voice barely a whisper. "Okay."

5

SARAH

It had been a few days since the last message, but the fear hadn't gone away. Every time I stepped outside, I felt like I was being watched. Every shadow seemed darker, every sound sharper. And though Ethan did his best to protect me, I couldn't shake the feeling that Stewart was lurking just beyond my line of sight, waiting for the perfect moment to strike.

I leaned back on the couch, trying to focus on the manuscript in front of me, but the words blurred together on the page. Writing used to be my escape, my sanctuary from the chaos of life. But now, it felt like even that was slipping away.

Ethan had been amazing—constantly checking in on me, staying close, and making sure I wasn't alone. But I could see the tension building in him. He was trying to hold it all together, but I knew he was just as scared as I was, even if he wouldn't admit it.

I sighed, running a hand through my hair. "This isn't working," I muttered to myself, pushing the laptop away.

Just then, the door creaked open, and Ethan stepped inside, his face tight with worry. He'd been out checking in with Mark, and the tension in his body told me that he hadn't gotten any good news.

"Everything okay?" I asked, my voice tentative.

Ethan's eyes softened as he looked at me. "Yeah. Just keeping an eye on things." He walked over to me, sitting on the edge of the couch. "Mark's fine. He's staying alert, and I made sure he's locking up tight at night."

I nodded, trying to take comfort in his words, but the knot of anxiety in my stomach didn't loosen.

Ethan reached out, brushing a strand of hair away from my face. "You're still worried, aren't you?"

I bit my lip, not wanting to admit just how terrified I really was. "It's just... I don't know how to make this go away. No matter what I do, Stewart's always there. I can't even write anymore. I can't focus."

Ethan's hand slid to my cheek, his thumb stroking gently across my skin. "You don't have to do this alone, Sarah. I'm here."

I nodded, leaning into his touch. "I know. But it's not enough, Ethan. I'm scared. He's out there, and I don't know what he'll do next."

"I won't let him hurt you," Ethan said firmly, his voice low and steady. "I swear."

I wanted to believe him, but deep down, I knew that this was beyond both of us. Stewart wasn't just any ex-boyfriend. He was dangerous, and no matter how much Ethan tried to protect me, I couldn't shake the feeling that something terrible was going to happen.

"We should go to the police," I said, though I knew it wouldn't help. "He's a dirty cop, but maybe there's something they can do..."

Ethan shook his head. "We've already been down that road. Until we have concrete evidence against him, they won't touch him."

I closed my eyes, feeling the weight of hopelessness press down on me. I couldn't live like this forever, constantly looking over my shoulder, waiting for the next threat. I had to find a way to end this, once and for all.

Suddenly, my phone buzzed again, pulling me from my thoughts. I glanced at the screen, expecting another taunt from Stewart, but this time it was Mark.

Hey, sis. I need you to meet me at the restaurant. It's urgent.

I frowned, reading the message twice. Mark never asked me to meet him out of the blue like this. Something felt off.

"What is it?" Ethan asked, noticing the change in my expression.

"It's Mark. He wants me to meet him at the restaurant. He says it's urgent."

Ethan's eyes narrowed, suspicion flickering across his face. "That doesn't sound right."

I swallowed hard, my heart pounding in my chest. "You think it's a trap, don't you?"

Ethan nodded grimly. "It could be. Stewart's been getting more desperate. He might be using Mark to lure you out."

A chill ran down my spine. I couldn't believe I was in this position—afraid to meet my own brother because of a psychopath's game.

"We need to be careful," Ethan said, standing up. "If Stewart's using Mark as bait, then we're going to turn the tables on him."

I stood as well, my mind racing. "What are you thinking?"

Ethan's jaw tightened, determination hardening his features. "We're going to confront Stewart. End this once and for all."

We drove to the restaurant in silence, both of us on edge. Ethan's hand never left mine, his grip firm and reassuring, but I could feel the tension thrumming through him. This wasn't just about protecting me anymore—it was about taking down a man who had terrorized me for too long.

When we pulled into the parking lot, my heart skipped a beat. There was no sign of Mark's truck. The restaurant was dark, the windows shuttered. Something was definitely wrong.

"Stay close to me," Ethan said, his voice low and authoritative. With the calm precision of a man who'd seen combat, he pulled his service weapon from the glove compartment—a piece of equipment he'd carried during his time as a Navy SEAL. Checking the safety and ensuring it was ready, he tucked it securely into his waistband.

His training kicked in, movements steady and controlled. This wasn't just some random act of bravado—Ethan knew exactly what he was doing. He'd been trained for situations like this, and while he wasn't in uniform anymore, the instincts to protect were hardwired into him.

My breath uneven as I followed him out of the car, every instinct screaming at me to run. But I couldn't leave Mark behind. If Stewart had done something to him, I would never forgive myself.

Ethan led the way, his body tense and alert as we approached the door. He tried the handle—it was unlocked.

"Stay behind me," he whispered, pushing the door open and stepping inside.

The restaurant was eerily quiet, the only sound the creak of the floorboards beneath our feet. My heart pounded in my ears as I clutched Ethan's arm, my eyes darting around the room, searching for any sign of Stewart—or Mark.

"Mark?" I called out softly, my voice shaking.

No response.

Ethan's eyes were sharp, scanning every shadow, every corner of the room. "Stay close," he whispered, his hand brushing against mine.

We moved deeper into the restaurant, the tension thickening with each step. But then, from the back of the room, I heard it—a faint noise, like the scuff of a shoe against the floor.

Ethan froze, his body going rigid as he turned toward the sound. He drew his gun, motioning for me to stay put. My heart raced as he crept forward, his movements silent and calculated, every step filled with purpose.

And then, out of the shadows, Stewart emerged.

My blood ran cold.

6

ETHAN

Stewart stepped into the light, his eyes gleaming with malice. He held a gun casually in his hand, twirling it like it was nothing more than a toy. But I knew better. One wrong move, and this could all end in disaster.

I felt Sarah tense behind me, her breath quivering as she saw him. I kept my body between her and Stewart, my grip tightening around the handle of my own gun. There was no room for mistakes.

"Well, isn't this a cozy little reunion," Stewart sneered, his voice dripping with disdain. "You thought you could just run off with my girl, huh, Ethan? You think you can just play the hero?"

I didn't respond. I wasn't here to play his games, and I wasn't about to give him the satisfaction of seeing me rattled.

"Where's Mark?" Sarah's voice was strong, but I could hear the underlying fear. She was scared, and I didn't blame her. Stewart was unpredictable, and that made him dangerous.

Stewart's grin widened. "Oh, he's around. Don't worry, sweetheart. He's safe—for now. But that all depends on you."

My blood boiled at the way he looked at her, like she was his possession. "This ends tonight," I said, my voice low and even. "You're not getting out of this, Stewart. It's over."

Stewart's laughter echoed through the empty restaurant. "You think you can stop me? I've got connections, Ethan. People who owe me favors. You can't touch me."

"Maybe not legally," I growled, stepping forward, "but that doesn't mean you're walking out of here."

Stewart's eyes flicked to Sarah, and I saw the moment he decided to escalate the situation. His gun shifted, aiming directly at her. My heart skipped a beat, but I was already moving.

With practiced precision, I raised my weapon and fired. The shot rang out, and Stewart's gun clattered to the floor as he stumbled back, clutching his arm. His face twisted in pain and anger, but I wasn't done.

In an instant, I was on him, disarming him and pinning him to the ground. The years of military training kicked in—every move calculated, every second vital.

"You're done," I hissed, pressing my knee into his back as he groaned beneath me.

Sarah rushed forward, her eyes wide with shock, but relief was written all over her face. "Is he... is it over?" she whispered, her voice trembling.

I nodded, holding Stewart down as he cursed and spat, his defiance still burning bright. "It's over. He won't hurt you again."

The police arrived within minutes, taking Stewart into custody. His threats and rants echoed in the air as he struggled against the officers. "This isn't the end!" he shouted. "I'll get out, and you'll regret this!" But as the handcuffs clicked around his wrists and he was dragged toward the waiting cruiser, I knew the threat had finally been neutralized.

Just as the chaos began to settle, one of the officers called out from inside the bar. "Hey, we found something. You better come take a look."

My heart dropped. I glanced at Sarah, whose face had gone pale, and together we hurried inside. The officer led us to the back storage room. There, in the dim light, we found Mark—tied up and gagged, slumped against the wall. My stomach clenched at the sight. He looked disoriented but alive, his eyes widening with relief as we rushed over.

"Mark!" Sarah gasped, falling to her knees beside him and quickly working to untie the ropes around his wrists. "Oh my God, are you okay?"

He coughed, rubbing his wrists as the ropes fell away, but managed a weak smile. "Yeah, I'll live. That bastard jumped me from behind. I couldn't stop him."

Stewart's charges just escalated. Kidnapping and attempted murder—he'd be going away for a long time.

"Let's get you out of here," I said, helping Mark to his feet.

The paramedics arrived to check on Mark, and as they led him outside, I turned to Sarah, who was watching as Stewart was loaded into the back of the police car. Her shoulders sagged with exhaustion, and I could see the weight of everything that had happened settling over her.

"It's really over," she whispered, her voice trembling like she didn't fully believe it.

I walked over to her, wrapping my arms around her and pulling her close. "Yeah, it's over. You're safe now."

She let out a shaky breath, burying her face in my chest. "I don't know what I would've done without you, Ethan."

"You don't have to worry about that anymore," I murmured, kissing the top of her head. "I'm not going anywhere."

We stood there for a long time, the reality of what had just happened sinking in. For the first time in weeks, there was no immediate threat hanging over us, no need to look over our shoulders. But there was still something I needed to do—something I had been thinking about since this all started.

Epilogue

Two weeks had passed since Stewart had been taken away. Sarah had moved back into her own place, but things had been different between us. Not in a bad way—far from it. We were closer than ever. The time we'd spent together had made it clear that I couldn't imagine my life without her. And I wasn't about to let her slip away again.

That's why I'd gone ahead with my plan.

As I pulled up to the little Airbnb where I'd been staying, I couldn't help but smile. Sarah loved this place. She'd mentioned it so many times—how it was the perfect spot for her writing, how peaceful and inspiring it was. It was more than just a temporary hideaway for us; it had become a sanctuary.

I'd taken the plunge. I bought the place. And now, I was ready for the next step.

I stood by the front door, the house keys jingling in my hand. But the key wasn't on any ordinary keychain—it was attached to an engagement ring. One I'd been carrying around for the past few days, waiting for the right moment.

And tonight, I knew the moment had come.

Sarah pulled up a few minutes later, stepping out of her car with a smile. She looked more relaxed than I'd seen her in weeks, and it made my heart swell. She deserved this—peace, happiness, safety. Everything.

"Hey," she said, walking over to me. "What's going on?"

I smiled, holding up the keys. "I've got a surprise for you."

Her eyes widened. "What is it?"

I handed her the keys, watching her expression carefully. "I bought the house. For us."

Her jaw dropped. "What? Ethan, you didn't—"

But then she noticed the keychain, her eyes catching the glint of the engagement ring. She froze, her breath hitching as she looked up at me, her hands trembling.

"Ethan..." she whispered, her voice barely audible.

I dropped to one knee, pulling the ring free from the keychain and holding it out to her. "Sarah, I've loved you since that night all those years ago. I left because of duty, but I'm done running. I want to be with you. Forever. Will you marry me?"

Tears filled her eyes as she nodded, her voice choked with emotion. "Yes. Yes, of course I will."

I slid the ring onto her finger, standing up to pull her into my arms. We kissed, the kind of kiss that was filled with promise, with the future we both deserved.

As we stood there, wrapped in each other's arms, I knew that everything we'd been through had brought us to this moment. And from here on out, there was nothing we couldn't face together.

I leaned down, pressing my lips to hers in a slow, lingering kiss. The kind of kiss that promised a future full of love, of laughter, of quiet mornings and long nights. The kind of kiss that told her I wasn't going anywhere.

When we finally pulled apart, Sarah glanced through the open front door, her gaze landing on the small writing desk I had set up for her by the window. Her eyes lit up, and I couldn't help but smile.

"You're going to write your book here," I said, watching as she moved toward the desk, her fingers brushing over the smooth surface. "You're going to tell your story."

She turned back to me, a soft laugh escaping her lips. "My life has felt like a novel lately."

I grinned. "Maybe it's time to write your happy ending."

The End

Did you like this book? Then you'll LOVE Saved by My Damaged Protector.

Snowed in with a brooding, ex-marine? I never stood a chance.

Stranded in the middle of a snowstorm, the last thing I expected was to be rescued by a rugged ex-Marine with eyes as dark as sin and a body made for sinning.

Monty's a gruff, no-nonsense guy, living alone to escape the demons of his past. But when he offers me shelter, the storm outside is nothing compared to the heat that builds between us inside.

Each stolen glance, every brush of his rough hands against my skin, makes it impossible to deny the raw, electric chemistry between us.

I know I should resist. He's a forbidden temptation, a man too broken for love. But one night is all it took for our desire to explode—fast, hard, and hotter than I ever imagined.

Just when I think I can walk away from our unforgettable time together, I'm hit with the shock of a lifetime—I'm pregnant.

Now, I must break through Monty's walls, get him to trust me to open his heart so we can finally share the future I never knew I wanted.

Click here now to get Saved by My Damaged Protector!
https://www.amazon.com/dp/B0DRKQYXJ3

7

SNEAK PEAK

Chapter 1 Monty

The snow is coming down hard as I head home after a quick trip into town for supplies, since I'll be trapped inside for at least a few days. That's the life I chose and I'm happy with it, but I need to eat and luckily, there weren't a lot of people to bother me in the closest town with decent stores for shopping.

Everyone is worried about the storm and doing everything they can to prepare for it. For me, it's just normal life.

I am rounding a corner when I see the back of a red vehicle in the air and a person pacing the snowy road.

What the fuck is going on?

I drive past slowly, taking in the scene as I consider what to do. I have no idea why this woman is out here on the road at all, and it looks like she's alone. As a son and brother, not to mention a former marine, I know I need to stop and offer help, and I pull over as I look around at the falling snow.

"Can I help?" I hop out of my SUV and look at her to see messy blond curls and red cheeks on a beautiful woman. "What happened?"

"I lost all navigation and ended up in this ditch. There is a meeting I need to get to, and I have no idea where I am." She crosses her arms and then looks around at nothing but snow and trees.

"What are you doing driving in this weather?" I can't help but ask, knowing I sound angry. I suppose I am. This isn't safe weather to be out in, much less driving.

"I was going to a meeting about a film location. I am the set location manager." Her eyes narrow as she looks at me, glancing away. I can tell she's frustrated and not from this area based on her thin sweatshirt and sneakers. Everyone here wears warm clothes and boots because we know better. "Is there a hotel nearby? I can just get a room until I can get back on the road."

"You're not getting out of here anytime soon. The storm is going to get worse, and a tow truck won't even come out here until it clears up. As far as a hotel, the nearest town is an hour away." I watch as her face falls, and she closes her eyes, cursing softly.

Do I want this woman I don't know in my cabin? No. I can't leave her here and hope that someone else finds her, since most people locked themselves inside of their homes and this is a remote area. My mom taught me better than that and as a former marine, I protected people.

"I have somewhere you can stay until a tow truck can come out. You're not going anywhere in this." Her eyes study me with a flash of fear in them, and I know I am an intimidating man. I take pride in that, but I can't leave this woman out here alone. "I won't hurt you. You'll be warm and fed. Safe."

"Where do you live?"

"About a mile down the road. I'm one of the people here that appreciate my privacy." I still see the hesitation in her eyes and sigh. "I have a mother and sisters that would never let me hear the end of it if I left you out here. How about you get your stuff, and we get out of the cold weather?"

She looks around at the falling snow which is steadily increasing and crosses her arms over her chest. She mutters something and turns to walk to the car, and I follow to make sure she doesn't fall down.

"I am just trying to keep you from breaking a leg." Holding up my hands, I pause as she gets into the car, awkwardly pulling a suitcase from the car, which I take. From there, she grabs a backpack and a purse. I offer to take the backpack, and she surrenders it to me with a sigh. "We might as well exchange names. I don't know how long this storm will last. I'll start. I'm Monty."

"Rita." She walks beside me and helps me load up my older Tahoe. "Why do you live out here? Are you alone in your place?"

"As I said, privacy. It's just me in my cabin." I start the engine, and heat fills the cab as she slumps against the seat. "You aren't from this area, are you?"

"I'm from Hollywood." That could be the worst place in the world to live for me and I turn the heat up. "This is nothing like what I'm used to. How do you not freeze to death?"

"Warm jackets and boots to start." I pull forward and drive to my house, as she warms up as far away from me in the car as possible. "You get used to it."

"I doubt that." I sense that she's tired and wonder when the accident happened since I've been in town for a couple of hours. "At least I'm not staying. At this point, I might not even have a job anymore."

I glance at her, wondering what company would punish her for wrecking her car in this weather. If they brought her out here in this, they probably don't care to begin with.

We reach my cabin in ten minutes, and I park near the door as Rita looks at it, frowning.

"It's bigger than I thought it would be."

"Did you think I lived in a shack or something?" I feel slightly offended but she's from California and likely doesn't understand remote living. "It has two bedrooms and two bathrooms along with everything else I need to survive."

"Is there a fireplace?" Hope fills her voice, and I look at her with a frown.

"I live in Montana. Of course."

We get out and Rita helps with her luggage while hurrying to the porch, shivering in the dropping temperature. I saunter over as she narrows her eyes, slowly unlocking the door before she runs inside.

"I'm going to unload some groceries. Make yourself at home." The door closes and I let out a long breath. I hope this weather clears up soon. I didn't plan for anyone being here.

Ever.

Her luggage is just inside the door when I walk in with bags, watching as she sits in front of the fire. I can get a better look at her now and she has pale blond hair that falls in soft curls around her face. Rita has a great body and I pause before stepping into the kitchen. It might be nice of she asked if I need help but what can I expect from a girl like that?

I take extra time putting everything away, which isn't that much considering there is now two of us here.

"Want me to make some coffee to warm you up?"

"Yes, please. I love coffee." Her voice is soft and sleepy, and I look at her for a moment before brewing some. It's late afternoon and coffee isn't the norm for me at this time of day but I'm going to be locked in this fucking cabin for at least a few days.

What else is there to do?

I ask if she takes cream or sugar, and Rita slowly stretches before making her way to my galley kitchen. Her eyes are a bright emerald green and not what I expected at all. She stands far away from me and stirs some milk and sugar into her cup, reading the labels with a sour expression.

"Problem?" I arch a brow, and she glances at me.

"I am normally low carb but whatever. I guess I can't be picky since I'm not freezing to death out there." She gestures to the kitchen window with a scowl.

She's one of those women that probably lives on salad and water though I suspect Rita is athletic on some level based on her lean frame. That and she probably starves herself unlike most women here. Not that I'd know since I keep to myself, apart from seeing my family a few hours away when I feel like

making the trip.

Rita walks back to the fire, sitting on my worn leather couch directly in from of the flames.

"I have a satellite phone if you need to call anyone. It's in case of an emergency." I sit at the end of the couch and watch as she sips her coffee.

"My phone broke when I crashed, and it has all the numbers in it. It wouldn't even come on." She looks at the clock and sighs. "I am already beyond late. It doesn't matter now."

"Who the hell do you work for? You got into an accident, and they wouldn't want to know? What about your family?" She jumps at the disbelief in my voice, setting her coffee down on the table beside her with trembling hands.

"My parents passed away in a car accident four years ago and they were it. No siblings. As far as my boss, it's all about getting the job done as fast as possible. It's what I thought I wanted to do for a long time." She pushes her hair back and blinks. "Listen to me. It's not like I'm never going home. How long do storms last around here?"

"It's January and the heart of winter. This is a bad one so who knows?" She looks at me with a hopeless expression for a moment. "I'm sorry about your family."

I couldn't imagine living without my large family even if I don't see them all the time. We just spent Christmas together a few weeks ago and it was as incredible as usual. I lived away from them for eight years when I joined the Marines and now that I have roots here in Montana, I don't want to leave them again.

"Thanks. It's-it's weird now that they are gone. Both were in the industry, and I thought I'd follow in their footsteps without the spotlight."

She's beautiful enough to be on screen but Rita said she worked as a set location manager. A background job. There's something about her that screams to me she wants to fade in the industry she chose.

I think about the vision of Hollywood and California I have. It's crowded and stifling. Nothing I want to be a part of. Even in the military, I never lived anywhere like that.

"Can I take a shower? I am still so cold and just want to stand under hot water." She turns to look at me and I nod, telling her where the bathroom is and that it's stocked with what she should need.

Rita thanks me and goes to her suitcase, rifling through it before taking some clothes into the hallway. Leaning back, I think about the undetermined amount of time Rita might be here. The storm was expected to be bad and the idea of anyone traveling here with that knowledge is beyond me.

I also can't be the man to send her out on her own with my childhood and military training.

She walks down the hall quietly and I watch her. There's a part of me that wants to comfort her after our conversation, but Rita seems like she needs some time alone.

What the fuck? Why am I thinking like that? I have made a point of living out here on my ranch completely away from civilization unless I went into town, women included. I haven't dated anyone since coming home and buying this cabin.

Just because I have a woman in my cabin for a few days doesn't mean I'm going to go soft and feed that need even though she's gorgeous. Rita might have someone at home waiting for her and since I barely know her, I have nothing to go on.

Something tells me Rita keeps to herself as much as I do, and I look back down the hall as the water starts in the bathroom. How much do I want to know?

Click here now to get *Saved by My Damaged Protector*
https://www.amazon.com/dp/B0DRKQYXJ3

Printed in Great Britain
by Amazon